To Jeanne

Love

From Dorothy

SCAMP and the BLIZZARD BOYS

SCAMP and the BLIZZARD BOYS

Dorothy Hamilton

Illustrated by James Converse

HERALD PRESS
Scottdale, Pennsylvania
Kitchener, Ontario
1980

Library of Congress Cataloging in Publication Data
Hamilton, Dorothy, 1906-
Scamp and the blizzard boys.
SUMMARY: When a blizzard causes Craig and his dog Scamp to take refuge with Doug and his mother, they all take precautions to survive the storm and then watch the community band together to help those in need.
[1. Blizzards—Fiction. 2. Community life—Fiction] I. Converse, James. II. Title.
PZ7.H18136Sc [Fic] 79-23670
ISBN 0-8361-1918-5
ISBN 0-8361-1919-3 pbk.

SCAMP AND THE BLIZZARD BOYS

Published simultaneously in Canada by Herald Press, Kitchener, Ont. N2G 4M5
Library of Congress Catalog Card Number: 79-23670
International Standard Book Numbers:
0-8361-1918-5 (hardcover)
0-8361-1919-3 (softcover)
Printed in the United States of America
Design: Alice B. Shetler

15 14 13 12 11 10 9 8 7 6 5 4 3 2 1

To
Douglas and Craig
who have a dog named
Scamp.

Chapter 1

DOUG HARTLEY rubbed a patch of steam from the window of the school bus. He couldn't see outside because snow was plastered against the window. *This must be a real bad storm, for them to let school out before lunch. All the other times they had us stay to eat what the cooks fixed.*

He raised up off the seat and looked toward the front of the bus. The windshield wipers were moving slowly, back and forth, back and forth. *They aren't doing a very good job. Probably because there's so much snow.*

His friend Craig leaned from his seat across the aisle. "What's a blizzard? Our teacher said we were going home because we were going to have a blizzard."

"It's a bad snowstorm, I *think.*"

"Oh! I never did hear that word," Craig said. "It sounds like gizzard to me. Or that big old bird that eats rabbits."

"Buzzard. We wouldn't be going home because of a gizzard or a buzzard."

"I know *that,*" Craig said. "Do you suppose we'll get out of going to school?"

"We're already out."

"I mean for a long time."

"I don't know."

"I hated to miss gym," Craig said. "I wish we'd had it the first thing instead of spelling."

Doug raised up again to see where they were. The snow was like a thick white cloud close to the earth. *I can't see past the side of the road. No trees or mailboxes or anything. Can Mr. Dwight?*

As Doug sat down the bus came to a stop. "You're home, Douglas," the driver said.

"See you, Craig. Call me if we get snowed in."

"You'll be snowed in all right," Mr. Dwight said. "We all will. I just hope we all get home first. You watch, boy. Keep your eye on the house. Walk straight to it."

Soft flakes melted on Doug's cheeks and clung to the sleeves of his blue hooded jacket as he headed slowly toward the house.

SCHOOL BUS
J 42
Converse

"Okay. 'Bye." The snow was thicker on Hickory Lane than it had been on the parking lot at Blue River Valley School. *But it's not too bad. Not even half way up on my boots.* Soft flakes melted on his cheeks and clung to the sleeves of his blue hooded jacket. *Man, this would be a great time to make a snowman—if Mom will let me.*

As he came to the porch he heard the sound of a car. *Only it's noisier than ours. Besides, I don't think mom would go anyplace now. Not with it snowing so hard.*

The chugging roar became louder and Doug turned to see a truck come down the driveway from the garage. *That's Uncle John's truck.*

"Hi," he called and waved so hard that a little shower of snow from his jacket sifted down, some falling on his face. *He didn't see me. Probably had to watch where he was going.*

He decided to ring the front doorbell. *No use to wade in snow all the way round to the back.*

His mother had the door open before the jangling sound stopped. "I've been pacing the floor waiting for you," she said. "I knew you were coming. Get in where it's warm."

"How did you know?"

"Two ways. Come to the kitchen where it's warmer. First, let me check to see if the storm door's latched. If the wind rises, as they say on the radio, it could blow it off the hinges."

"Is that how you found out that they were letting school out? On the radio?"

"That's one way. Your teacher also had her aide call all the parents to be sure they'd be home."

"What if some aren't?"

"She said she'd keep them at school until the parents are located. Did you notice? Did anyone stay?"

"I don't know. They hurried us out real fast, almost like when it's a fire drill. Say, Mom, why did you shut that door between the rooms?"

"Because the blizzard's supposed to come from the northwest. This front part of the house will be hard to heat. Besides, we'll be a lot warmer in the kitchen now—no matter what happens."

How does Mom know so much about blizzards? I guess from hearing Grandpa Bill. She probably listens better than I do when he talks about olden times.

"Wait! Before we go to the kitchen let's head upstairs and grab some blankets and pillows. I turned the heat low up there. So leave your coat on."

"Mom, why are we doing all this?" Doug asked. "Are you scared?"

"No, not afraid. I just want us to be prepared—in case your dad doesn't get home. We'll have to take care of each other."

"You think Dad won't come?"

"He might not be able to get here. Your Uncle John said he wanted to get home before the wind comes up and drifts the snow. He had a little trouble getting out his lane with the load of wood."

Load of wood? Doug thought. *Where was he going with wood?*

Doug followed his mother up the stairs. He couldn't hear all of what she said because she kept ahead of him. And she couldn't hear him very well either. He said, "I didn't see any wood on Uncle John's truck. Why would he bring it here anyway?"

"Oh, Douglas, I'm not explaining things to you. I just keep running from one thing to another. Just like I have all day since the storm warning came on television. Here, take these. Go down to the kitchen and I'll make us some hot chocolate and tell you what's going on."

Doug had trouble seeing over the top of the three feather pillows. He had to feel around with his foot for the edge of the steps. *But I guess it wouldn't hurt much if I fell on these pillows. Not if Mom didn't come tumbling after me.*

When he reached the swinging door which opened into the kitchen, he turned around and bumped it open with his hip. Warm air came to meet him. He felt it on the back of his neck. Before he turned around he heard a different sound, different from any he'd ever heard in his house. *It's like when Grandpa Bill boils maple syrup and puts big sticks of wood on the fire.*

He dumped the pillows on a chair before he turned around. "Mom—you've put up the old stove. The one that was in the back porch."

"Yes. I've never wanted to throw it away. Your dad's teased me about clinging to the past. But I've never felt safe depending on an electric light wire for heat. Not when winds begin to howl and fill the roads with drifted snow so repair trucks couldn't get to us."

"Did Uncle John help you put up the pipe and move it in here?"

"No. I did this myself. The stove's light, made of

what they call sheet metal. And when I heard the forecast I went to New Castle and bought stovepipe and groceries. But why don't I tell you about that later? We have things to do. *Then* we'll have hot chocolate."

"We do?"

"Yes indeed," Ann said. "We need to bring in a good supply of wood, for one thing. It's in the shed behind the garage. I moved the lawn mower and other tools to the other half of the garage. Now, let's carry a supply to the back porch."

"Why? It's not far to that shed."

"Doug! We may not be able to get out there by morning. Put on another jacket. The temperature's dropped twelve degrees in an hour."

The wind swirled snow against Doug's face as he stepped away from the corner of the house. It seemed to take his breath, and blow him sideways. He left his mother pile sticks on his outstretched arms. "Now they're as high as your chin," she said. "That's enough for you to carry, especially in this wind."

After eight trips between the garage and the back porch the stack of wood filled all the empty space. "I'll bring in two more armloads and put them behind the stove. You go on in and spread newspapers and get warm."

Doug's legs felt stiff and his cheeks stung like there were cold needles in them. He took off his snow-crusted gloves and held his hands over the stove. His mother had put the copper teakettle on the flat top and steam curled from the curved spout.

As he went to the magazine rack in the living room he thought, *Maybe I'm a little scared. But not much. It's kind of like being a pioneer. Only this isn't a log cabin. Or there aren't any Indians or* buffaloes. *Or were there ever any of them in Indiana? I'll have to ask someone about that.*

Chapter 2

WHEN Doug's mother came into the kitchen she sank down on a chair. "That's work," she said. "I'm out of breath. But I think we have enough wood to last several days."

"Days? Do you think we'll be here by ourselves that long?"

"We could be. I keep thinking your dad will call from wherever he is—if he can. He'll worry about us."

Doug looked at his mother's face and thought, *Is she worried about Dad? Or us?*

"There's another idea in my mind," she said. "I'll get the yardstick when I get these snowy boots off my feet."

Doug watched as she put her brown boots on folded newspapers. *It's like Mom knows how to do things in a blizzard. She always seems to know what to do no matter what happens.*

She opened the door on the front of the stove and stepped toward the low stack of wood against the wall. "I like to look at live coals," she said. "They have a rosy glow and little fingers of flame curl upward."

Doug moved closer and watched sparks fly when the two sticks of firewood were shoved through the door. The sparks danced in the air and were soon gone.

"What do you want to do with the yardstick, Mom?"

"I'm going to measure the hall that goes down to the den. I'm wondering if two mattresses for twin beds would fit there end to end."

"You mean we'd sleep down here? Is that why we went for pillows and blankets?"

"Not exactly. At first I thought we'd sleep on the sofa bed in the den, or move it to the end of the kitchen. But it's so heavy. Twin bed mattresses would be easier to move."

"Are we going to do it now?"

"Let me think about it. There's still time. First I'll hook the lead-in wire to the portable TV when I get it moved to the kitchen desk. We can move mattresses after we eat. Are you—well now! That's a silly question. When weren't you hungry when you got home from school? And after all that wood carrying you're probably starved."

"We don't have a very good place to sit to watch TV," Doug said. "Except on straight chairs."

"Well, why don't you pull two more comfortable ones in from the den? My small swivel rocker and your beanbag chair or whatever you want."

When Doug walked into the den he could hear the windows shaking. The wind made a whistling sound that was a little like a train whistle. *That's cause this room's on the north side I guess.* He shivered as he pulled the second chair through the hall.

"Push hard on that door," his mother said. "Then put this folded rug along the crack at the bottom."

"What are we going to have to eat?" Doug asked.

"Well, I chose potato soup. There's something about a cold night that makes it seem right. Probably because my own mother often made it in snowy weather. Look in the refrigerator or on the cabinet shelves. What else looks good to you?"

When Doug opened the refrigerator door he said, "Mom! The shelves are stuffed full."

"I know. I went to the store early when I first heard about the blizzard. I spent all next week's grocery money as well as this week's. I felt like a squirrel storing up food."

"Could we have hot dogs? They're good in any weather."

As Doug's mother poured milk into the pan in which diced potatoes and onions bubbled, the telephone rang. "I'll get it, Mom." Before he could answer he heard his father saying, "Ann? You there?"

"It's me, Dad."

"Doug. You all right?"

"We're fine. Where are you?"

"I'm up here in Wabash in a motel. Stuck. May I speak to your mom? You sure you're all right?"

"We're great, Dad."

Doug sat down in his brown bean bag chair which he'd pulled close to the wood-burning stove. He listened to what his mother said and tried to figure out his dad's part of the conversation. *Seems like they're mostly trying to tell each other not to worry.*

"Charles," his mother said, "I know you never wanted me to do this, but I set the wood stove up here in the kitchen. Yes. . . . John brought me a load of wood. Had a little trouble getting here." She told about moving things to the kitchen and going to the store for food and a stovepipe. "Now if the electricity goes off we'll be warm and fed. . . . That's right. There's less danger of the telephone getting out of order. The cable's are underground. But don't worry if you can't get us. *You* take care. Don't start home until you're sure it's safe."

As Doug's mother turned from the wall extension phone she said, "But he will worry. He was in that conference and didn't hear the weather forecast until it was already unwise to start home. But he did make it as far as Wabash, to a motel.

"As soon as we've finished," Doug's mother said as they ate, "we'll fill plastic jugs with water. Then we'll run the bathtub full and whatever else I can find. If the power goes off the pump won't run. I've already gathered up every candle in the house and checked to see if my mother's old lamp had any oil in it."

"You sure have thought of a lot of things," Doug said as he reached for three Butter-crisp crackers.

"I've been busy all right. I haven't had a spare moment all day. I haven't even talked to anyone on the telephone except Virginia Scott. She called just before you came. She was in New Castle and wanted to know if I needed anything. I hope she got home—Oh, Doug, was Craig on the bus?"

"Sure. Why?"

"I'm going to check. What if that boy—"

I know what Mom's thinking even if she doesn't say it. She's afraid Craig's mom might be stuck somewhere in her little car and that he might be home by himself. Doug's throat felt tight, like something was stuck in it.

"The line's busy. I hope that means Ginny's home. But I'm going to keep trying."

Before she sat down at the table the telephone rang. Doug listened until he heard her say, "Oh, Ginny, that's terrible. No wonder you're frantic. But you're safe now. Let me think who we can call. I'll tell you what. You call me back from the park shelter house as soon as you get the line. Keep trying."

"Craig's by himself," Doug said. "Right?"

"Yes. His mother was stuck in a line of cars on State Road 3. And a tow truck pulled them one by one into the park."

"What's going to happen to Craig?"

"I'm trying to think. I don't dare try to get there. Even if it is only a quarter of a mile. What do you call those cars that travel through snow better?"

"Four-wheel drives."

"Who has one?"

"I don't know of anyone," Doug said.

"I'm going to call John."

Doug walked to the window. He couldn't see anything but snow that had been plastered against the screen. *Is Craig scared? I sure would be.* He turned when he heard his mother say, "You think he'd try it then? Fine. I'll call Craig and tell him to be ready. *Certainly* we want him here."

"Who has a four-wheel drive?"

"No one close. But Jeff Sanders has a snowmobile. He lives in the trailer across from John."

"I know him. He's a runner on the track team. He jogs past here a lot."

"Well I hope we're not risking his safety. But we have to try."

"Are you sure Jeff will do it?"

"Your Uncle John's going to see him and come along."

"Mom! Three people can't ride on a snowmobile."

"I know. John will stay at Scott's and check on the furnace—that is he will if they make it. The wind's blowing harder all the time. Now, we must call Craig."

"Could I?"

"Yes. But let me talk to him too."

When Craig answered Doug said, "Hey, why didn't you call me when you were by yourself?"

" 'Cause I went to sleep watching TV and didn't know it was getting dark outside."

He's been crying. I can tell, Doug thought. "Wait a minute. My mom wants to tell you something good."

Chapter 3

DOUG stood close to the telephone while his mother talked to Craig. "Now listen," she said. "Get on your warmest clothes and be ready. My brother and his neighbor are going to come for you and bring you here—on a snowmobile. . . . You like that idea don't you? Bring some pajamas and anything else you think you'll need."

As his mother listened Doug turned the backyard light on and looked out the window. Snow was swirling around and around. *Looks like it never lands on the ground. But it does or it wouldn't be getting deeper.*

"Fine," he heard his mother say. "Bring him along. You couldn't leave him there. Now don't be afraid. Your mother's safe. She's already told you that. And she'll be calling here to see if you're all right.

"That poor child," Ann Hartley said as she hung the receiver on the hook. "He's frightened. Things like this should never happen. How could it if the teachers called to be sure someone was at home? Why don't you turn on the TV? Let's see what they're saying about the storm."

Doug watched as his mother washed the dishes and filled jugs with water. "That's all they're talking about on every channel," he said. "Stuff about the weather, and pictures of stuck cars."

His mother sat down and watched with him until the announcer said, "The full force of the wind will not be felt here until nine o'clock."

"That's one good thing. John and Jeff will not be out in the very worst. They'll be able to get Craig and Scamp here and get home themselves first. By the way, who's Scamp?"

"He's Craig's dog."

"Is he big?"

"No, not very. About like Aunt Fran's poodle, only it isn't—not a poodle, I mean."

"That's good. There might not be room on the snowmobile for a collie or a shepherd."

"Or a Great Dane."

Doug's mother decided to bring the mattresses

from the guest bedroom. She said there wasn't any sense to drag some from upstairs.

"I'll help," Doug offered.

When they opened the door into the front rooms cold air came to meet them, and the roaring sound of wind was all around them. "Is the heat off already?"

"No. But I turned it down to forty," his mother said. As they went toward the bedroom Doug stepped on something soft. He looked down and saw a ridge of snow from the front door.

"It's blowing in the cracks. I'll double a rug against them."

"I never saw snow drift inside a house before," Doug said.

"I have many times. You get on that end and hold this mattress upright. We'll drag and push it through the rooms and then return for the other one."

By the time the puffy mattresses were end to end in the long hall Doug was beginning to be more worried about Craig. *Shouldn't he be here by now? Mom called Uncle John a long time ago. At least it seems like it.* When the phone rang, Doug's throat felt tight again. *Is something wrong?* He breathed easier when he realized his mother was talking to Mrs. Scott.

"Yes. He should be here anytime now. I expected you to call before now. . . . I see. How many people

Craig hugged Scamp tight as Jeff drove the snowmobile into the swirling snow and headed toward Doug's house.

converse

are in the shelterhouse? Thirty? No wonder the phone's been busy. Well—call back when you can."

As Doug's mother left the telephone she said, "I think I'll make hot chocolate now. Jeff may take time for a warm drink with us, and I can send a thermos full along for John. It's a good thing I bought extra milk for us, and now for Scamp."

Is she worried? Doug thought. *Is she afraid Uncle John and Jeff might not get to Craig's house? What would happen to them if they got stranded in the storm?*

Before he could ask the questions which were in his mind his mother turned the television set off. "I think I heard something. A new sound was added to the storm noises."

As she opened the door Doug heard bumping sounds. "Come in—don't worry about tracking snow. You all right?"

"We're okay," the tall young man said. "We had a little trouble seeing when the wind picked up. But we made it."

Doug walked over to his friend and said, "I'll help you. Let me take that satchel."

Craig grinned. "I'd better unzip my jacket. Old Scamp is wiggling around worse than ever."

"I wondered why you looked so fat. It's not clothes. It's dog."

"Yeah." Craig leaned closer to Doug. "You think your mom cares if we're here?"

"No, she'd care more if you were home by yourself. That was scary."

"I know. It really was."

Jeff stood at the door while he took gulps of the

hot drink. "I'd better not sit down. John's back there waiting. And it's not getting any calmer out there. That's for sure."

"I can't tell you how much we appreciate this," Doug's mother said. "Craig's mother is frantic with worry and to tell you the truth, so was I."

"Well, it's not that big a thing," Jeff said. "I might even be doing myself a favor. I wanted to spend some of the money I earned to buy a snowmobile. Now that the one the neighbor left with us when he went to Arizona came in so handy, my dad and mother may change their minds and let me get one of my own."

"Now you call, either you or John, when you get home."

"We will. You got enough stuff to eat?" Jeff asked.

"Yes. I stocked up this morning."

"Okay. When the wind dies down, call me if you run out. I'll be scooting around anyway, whether I have an excuse to or not."

Craig walked over the wood-burning stove after he'd hung his clothes on hooks in a corner. "Man this is neat. The warm comes out to meet you."

"Did you eat?" Doug's mother asked.

"Yes, before I went to sleep. Peanut butter sandwiches and orange juice. Mom's note said she'd be back from the store soon. But when she didn't come, I went to sleep."

"She'll be calling as soon as she can," Doug's mother said. "Now I'm going to make up my bed in the den on the couch. I'll have to walk on your sleeping places to get there. I must remember if I get up in the night not to step on you."

She's trying to get us to laugh, Doug thought. *It's like she's more worried than I am. Things seem okay now. It's kind of like an adventure—to me. I never was in a blizzard before.*

The two boys watched television for a few minutes. "You like to see all that storm stuff?" Doug asked.

"No. What else could we do?"

"I was thinking we could maybe play with my race track, but there's not much room for it out here. How about building some more to our Lego city."

"Okay."

When Doug's mother came stepping over the mattresses Doug said, "What if the heat does go off, Mom. You'd get cold in there, wouldn't you?"

"I can make a bed with chairs. Besides, I'll need to put wood in the stove more often."

Doug was beginning to feel sleepy. The warmth of the stove and the crackling sound of the burning wood made him feel safe. *I can hear the wind but it's not whistling and roaring back here like it was at the front of the house. That's probably because it's from the northwest, like Mom said.*

The telephone rang and Scamp, Craig's brown and black dog, ran from behind the stove and began to bark. "Be quiet!" Craig said. "He does that every time when he's in the house."

"I have a feeling that's your mother," Ann said. "Why don't you answer?"

Doug got up and sat on a chair at the table. He heard Craig tell his mother three times, "Sure, I'm fine. It's real warm here." He'd listen then say the same thing over. He told about the ride on the snowmobile. "It was really neat, Mom. Jeff said he might take me another ride when this blizzard's past. Me and Doug and Scamp. . . . Sure I brought him. Mrs. Hartley said I couldn't leave him by himself. . . . Okay. Okay." As he turned from the wall he said, "She wants to talk to you."

"She's crying," Craig said as he sat down across the table from Doug. "I don't know why. Everything's okay now."

"Sometimes that's when Moms cry."

"I know."

Chapter 4

GETTING UP from the floor beside the stove made Doug feel wide awake. He reached for an orange, peeled it, and divided it in three parts. Before he could ask his mother if she wanted a share of it, the telephone rang again. He could tell by listening that it was his aunt Lois. "Oh, I'm glad he's back," Doug's mother said. "Did they have any trouble?"

When she came to the table she said, "Jeff and

John couldn't see the edges of the road all the time. But it didn't make that much difference. The side ditches are full of snow and sometimes they crossed yards," she said as she pulled a section from her piece of the orange, "Didn't I hear you mention your race track?"

"Yes, but it's sort of crowded in here."

"Well, I think we're going to be here for a day or two, maybe longer. So why don't we clear off this table and move it to the end of the kitchen with the chairs and TV?"

"You mean we could set up the track and leave it? Where will we eat?"

"We can bring out the folding card table." As she put fruit and the syrup pitcher in the refrigerator she said, "Many times I've wished this kitchen was smaller, especially when it needs scrubbing. But now I'm glad it's big. We have room to make ourselves really comfortable. I think I'll begin hooking a rug. I'm not one bit sleepy."

"Me neither," Doug said. "Not like I was. Are you, Craig?"

"Not me. I had that long nap."

As Doug's mother came back from the den with her handiwork supplies the telephone rang again. And in the next hour she talked to three people.

"I guess everyone wants to know if everyone's all right," Doug said.

"Could be they don't have anything else to do."

"Could be."

The boys opened the drop leaves of the table and put curved and sloping sections of track together. They had time for four races before ten o'clock."

"I'm going to watch the news for a few minutes," Doug's mother said. "You should get ready for bed, shouldn't you? Do you want to take baths—oh, you can't. The tub's full of water."

"We could swim, Mom."

"Well, if the lights are still on in the morning we'll hurry through with the scrubbing of you two."

"Oh, I forgot," Craig said. "Mom said to tell you Scamp doesn't ever get to sleep in the house—unless it's thundering. Then he's scared."

"Where could he sleep?" Doug's mother asked. "Do you think he'd be warm enough in the back porch? There's a little heater out there to keep the water softener from freezing."

"That's better than his bed at home," Craig said. "It's in the garage."

"I'll get you a box from the basement," Doug's mother said. "And there's an old sweatshirt in the bathroom closet—in the rag bag."

Craig picked his dog up from behind the stove. "Come on, Scampie. We'll get you all fixed up."

"Let's put the box on the other side of the stack of wood," Doug said. "Then if snow comes through the crack in the door he won't get any on him."

"It sure is blowing hard," Craig said. "Sounds worse out here."

"That's cause the roof's tin and the walls aren't as thick maybe."

"Bring in as many sticks of wood as you can carry," Doug's mother said from the door. "That should last us all night."

"What did they say on TV about the storm?" Doug asked.

"About the same. Wind gusts up to forty or fifty miles an hour. Snow all night."

"Is that bad? Forty miles an hour?" Craig asked.

"Not so bad it couldn't be worse. I imagine we'll be surprised when daylight comes. Drifts will be high. The world will have a different look."

"You going to bed now, Mom?" Doug asked as he came from the bathroom.

"No. I'm going to move my chair close to the desk, so the light won't be in your eyes, and read awhile."

I think she wants to stay out here with us, Doug thought. *Does she think we're scared? Or is she?*

The boys decided to sleep so their feet would meet. Neither wanted the other to kick him in the face. They talked for a few minutes. Craig was concerned about where his mother would sleep. "They wouldn't have cots in the park shelterhouse," he told Doug. "Just hard park benches. I should have asked. But she kept asking about *me.*"

Doug turned over with his face to the wall. He put out one hand. Was it shaking a little? He moved to the middle of the mattress just as the telephone rang. He sat up so he could hear better. *That's Dad. I'd know even if Mom didn't keep saying Charles. She sounds different when she talks to him. Different in a nice way—like she talks to me.*

"Is the motel crowded?" Doug heard her ask. "Four to a room? Well, we're doing a little better than that. There are only three in here." She explained how Craig had been brought from his home and that people were checking to see if they were all right. "That's probably why you couldn't get us. I do feel safer knowing they buried the telephone cable last summer."

The last thing Doug's mother said before she put the telephone on the hook was, "Don't take *any* risks to get here. We're fine."

"I guess Dad wishes he'd got home," Doug said.

"Like my mom," Craig said.

"Just so everybody's where it's warm."

"Like us," Craig said.

Doug was pulling the two blankets over his shoulders when he felt a rush of cold air on his face and arms. Had a window blown out? He hadn't heard any glass breaking. He ducked his head when he felt the brush of fur on his face. "You have a bed-fellow," his mother whispered from the end of the hall. "Is Craig asleep?"

"I guess so. Why'd you let Scamp in?"

"Because. He kept whimpering."

"Was he cold?"

"I doubt it. The wind was making that tin roof rumble. I could hear it from here when the kitchen was quiet."

"He probably thought it was thunder," Doug said. "Come on, little dog. Lie down. It doesn't thunder during a blizzard. At least I don't think it does."

Scamp sniffed at Doug's hand then turned and went to the mattress where Craig slept. "He knows where he belongs," Doug's mother whispered. "Good night, Douglas. I'm going to step along the side to the other room. Call me if you want any-thing."

"You too. 'Night, Mom."

It seems like I wouldn't feel so safe, Doug

thought as he thumped his pillow to make it fluffier. *It's an awful bad storm, a real for sure blizzard. Dad's gone. And Craig's mom can't get home. Maybe a lot of people are out in the cold.*

He raised his head and saw that Scamp was curled up at Craig's feet. For a reason he didn't understand he sat up, reached down, and shook one of his friend's feet. Craig opened his eyes and said, "Hey! What—"

"Look beside your legs. You've got company."

Craig smiled. Doug could see his face in the glow from the lamp on the desk. "Mom said Scamp was scared of the wind noise."

"Come on, Scampie. You're okay," Craig said.

I'd be like him, Doug thought. *If I was in someone else's house, without either Mom or Dad, I'd want my dog close to me—if I had one.*

Before he went to sleep he thought about Craig's dad. *Craig almost never talks about him anymore. Not like he did when Mr. Scott first moved to wherever he went. I wonder where that is? Is there a blizzard there? Looks like he'd hear about how it is here and try to find out if Craig's okay. Even if he's mad at Mrs. Scott, it seems like he'd want to know about his own boy. Dad would. He'd always care what happens to me. Like he's already called home twice and that costs a lot of money—calling that far.*

Doug raised up again and looked to see if Craig was covered with the blanket. He saw one of Scamp's ears twitch as he slept. *If Dad called now, Mom could say that four of us are sleeping in this motel room, just like where he is.*

Chapter 5

WHEN Doug opened his eyes the next morning he didn't know where he was for a minute or two. He saw bare walls, not his bulletin board with the paper model of the Mayflower he'd made at school and the autographed picture of Kent Benson, the basketball player who grew up in New Castle.

Then he heard a banging sound and crawled toward the end of the mattress. His mother was shoving a stick of wood into the stove. He could see the red of the fiery coals. *I wonder if the blizzard's stopped?* He looked toward Craig's end of the hallway bed. *He must be asleep. I can't see anything but his hair.* Doug scooted from under the covers and whispered. "Is it still bad outside?"

"I think the wind's died down a little," his mother said. "There's not so much rumbling and roaring. I went to the front part of the house for a book and your transistor with the earplugs."

"Do they say anything about the blizzard on it?"

"That's all they're talking about. Roads are closed everywhere. Even city streets. All kinds of things are canceled or postponed, even basketball games. That's usually the last thing to be called off in Indiana."

"I guess the lights didn't go off," Doug said.

"Not here. But they were out an hour or more over by Oakville."

"Are you scared, Mom?"

Doug hadn't meant to ask that question. In a way he didn't want to know if his mother was afraid. If she was, he would be.

"No, not this morning. Last night and all day yesterday I felt some fear about what was ahead. But things always seem worse at night. And with your father gone I felt more responsible."

"Because you had to take care of me?"

"Because—well, at first I felt I had to take care of both of us. Then Craig came—and Scamp—and there were four. But this morning it's more like we're all in this together doing what each of us can."

Doug grinned. "What can Scamp do, Mom?"

"Who knows? But for now Craig's probably glad he's here."

Doug didn't say anything. All at once he was remembering Ott. He could almost see him, trotting along with his fluffy black tail swinging back and forth and his long ears sort of bouncing as he moved. He was the best old dog anyone could ever have.

"You're thinking about Ott, aren't you?" his mother asked.

Doug nodded.

"I do too. I've wished over and over that we'd have found the place where he was caught in the fence."

"Seems like we would've," Doug said. "We looked and looked. So did lots of other people."

"I know. I guess we didn't think he'd go so far away from home. Perhaps we didn't realize that when Ott saw a rabbit he'd chase it as long as it ran, even into the thick woods."

As Doug walked to the door he thought, *I didn't feel like crying this time when we talked about Ott. Is that because the bad time is further away? I don't want to forget him, not ever. Remembering, then, hurt a lot worse than it does now.*

He rubbed steam from the window but still couldn't see very far. "Mom, did you look? The snow's piled as high as the carport roof."

"I saw. But there's a little space outside the door. I think the shrubbery caught the snow and so the drifts are a few feet from the back step."

As they looked, Craig came up behind them and Scamp sniffed at Doug's feet. "Good morning,

Craig," Ann Hartley said. "You sleep good?"

"Yes'm. So did Scampie. Do you think we could let him outside?"

"Well, if you watch. Don't let him go far."

"Mom, he can't."

"Well, you boys get dressed. Or would you rather take a bath before you eat?"

Craig looked at Doug. "I'd always rather eat first."

"Me too."

"This is a good morning for hot cakes," Doug's mother said.

"Just about any morning's a good one for them," Craig said. "We don't have them anymore. My dad was the one who cooked them on Sundays."

"You two can dress, or would it be better to eat in your pajamas? So you don't have to dress again after the bath."

Doug had reached for his jeans and fuzzy sweat shirt. As he put them back on a chair he said, "Looks like we're not going to get out of the bath business. Dressing once is the best we can do. May I turn on the TV and watch cartoons?"

He clicked the knob all the way around twice. "Nothing's on but blizzard stuff," he said.

"Well, stop on one channel," his mother said. "See what they are forecasting."

The boys watched from the bean-bag chair and the swivel rocker. They saw long lines of semi-trailers stuck on a highway. Another shot showed empty streets with piles of snow. One announcer was in a motel lobby where people were sleeping on couches and in chairs. "My dad's in a place like that," Doug said. "Only he had a room with three other people. Strangers."

"I don't know where mine is," Craig said. " 'Less he's still in Indianapolis, like he was when it was my birthday."

"That's where the things we're seeing are happening."

"I know."

The telephone rang as the boys began to eat breakfast and three more times before Doug's mother finished her meal.

"That's Dad," Doug whispered when his mother answered the first time. "I can tell because she keeps saying we're fine. No one else would ask that many times."

The next two people who called asked how they were, but not so many times. "Your Aunt Lois and Uncle John wanted to check on us," Doug's mother said as she reheated a hot cake. "And Mrs. Burch up the road."

"I'll answer it," Doug said as the fourth call came. A man's voice came through crackling sounds. "This the Hartley place?"

"Yes sir."

"Your folks there?"

"My mom is."

"Put her on, boy."

"Some man wants you," Doug said. "Not Dad."

Craig stood up as Ann Hartley said, "Yes, Mr. Scott, Craig's here. Want to talk to him?"

It seemed to Doug that his friend had hold of the telephone before his mother finished asking the question. "Dad? It's me. How'd you know? . . . Oh, 'cause no one answered at home, huh? Well, no one's there."

Craig listened for a while, then he told how Jeff and Doug's uncle had brought him on the snowmobile. "I wasn't scared at home alone. Not very long anyway. 'Cause I was asleep most of the time." He explained that his mother was stuck and had to stay all night in the shelter house. "She went for groceries, Dad. For us. Because we'd be snowed in, only she's snowed out. . . . Sure! It's neat here. Doug's mom put up a stove. Like in olden times. And Scamp's here. You ought to see him. He's a lot bigger than on my birthday. . . . Okay. Okay."

As Craig came to the table he was smiling, but his eyes were misty. "He was really worried about us. About me anyway. He said he'd come for me if he could get here, and take care of me up home."

"How could he get here?"

"I don't know. Guess he didn't either. He talked about a bulldozer if he could find one somewhere. Is it okay if I eat another hot cake? I'm hungrier now."

"Certainly," Ann said. "Let me fry a couple more for you."

"Hey," Doug said. "We forgot about Scamp."

Craig ran to open the door, and his dog came scampering across the room. The snow on his paws made him slip on the floor. He ran to the back of the stove and curled up in a ball. "He knows where the warmest place is already, Mrs. Hartley," Craig said. "He's a pretty smart old dog."

Like Ott was, Doug thought.

Chapter 6

DOUG'S MOTHER turned on the television. "I think I'll see what they have to say about the weather," she said as she sat down in her swivel rocker. "You finish your breakfast." Doug heard part of the many things the announcer said, things like snowplows being stalled, cars stuck, airplanes being grounded, and buses not running.

"Looks like no one's going anywhere today," Craig said.

"We don't need to," Doug said. "We're okay here. What do you want to do? *After* we take baths."

"I don't know. Watch cartoons maybe? If they quit talking about the blizzard."

"I got a bunch of games. We can decide about that later."

"Suppose we could go outside?" Craig asked.

"I heard that," Ann Hartley said as she turned the television off. "If the wind dies down, we might see how far you could go. And where the drifts are. They're predicting that the high winds will be out of this area by early afternoon."

The telephone rang so many times that Doug's mother said *she* didn't have to worry about what *she* could do. "If I get a noon meal cooked, I'll be surprised."

Craig looked up every time he heard the ring. *He thinks it's his mother,* Doug thought. Just before they sat down to eat creamed chipped beef on hot biscuits Mrs. Scott finally did get through. She talked to Ann Hartley, then to Craig, and again to Doug's mother. As they finished their meal Craig said, "Mom was scared the phone wasn't working when it was busy all the time."

"I can imagine how she felt. I'd have been anxious too."

"How do those people eat?" Doug asked as he split another fluffy biscuit in half. "The people in the park shelterhouse."

"Mom told me," Craig said. "A man who runs a hamburger stand on up the state road couldn't get home. So a guy who builds houses and had something called an earthmover took sandwiches and coffee and fruit pies to the park."

"So! He was a *pie* mover," Doug said. "Right?"

"Right. And a sandwich mover."

"Your mother told me the same man hauled cots from the armory. A lot of people are trying to help others," Doug's mother said.

"Like you're helping me and Scamp," Craig said.

"Listen," Ann Hartley said. "You're helping us. Doug and I might be feeling very sorry for ourselves if we were the only ones here. In fact, I'd suggest that anyone who's about to be snowed in find two ten-year-old boys to keep them company." She smiled and added, "I'm serious. You don't see this as a bad time, do you?"

"No, not after I found out Mom was okay," Craig said. "And after my dad called."

"Me neither," Doug said. "It's an adventure, like in a book. Jeff and Uncle John rescued Craig and Scamp, and you put up the stove, and we got ready to keep warm."

"That's what I mean," his mother said. "There's nothing like two ten-year-olds to make going through a blizzard seem less frightening."

"I guess that makes us blizzard boys," Craig said. "Only I don't want to be one forever."

"Me neither," Doug said.

The wind seemed to die down all at once after two o'clock. It wasn't rumbling the roof anymore when the boys went to the back porch for firewood. Craig rubbed frost from the window and looked out into the yard. "You can see trees and the garage, but not the fence. It's covered by drifts. But the snow's not blowing."

"Couldn't we go outside now?" Doug asked as they piled sticks of wood behind the stove.

"Well, I'll go out with you. To see how the world looks," his mother said. "To see where it's safe for you to play."

They found a narrow path made because the snow had piled up against shrubbery along the carport. They walked in it single file until they could see the driveway and out toward the road. "Man!" Craig said. "Look at those drifts. They're like white mountains. You can't even see your garage. 'Cept some of the roof."

The air was cold and still. "Let's listen," Doug's mother said. "If a motor's running anywhere we can hear it when the air is crisp like this and when there's a cushion of snow on the ground."

"Some cushion!" Doug said. "It's more like a mattress—or a big stack of them."

"Nothing's moving for miles around," his mother said. "In a way it's like a great peacefulness. I think I'll go in now. But you must *not* go any farther than this. For one reason it's cold—almost down to zero. And for another you might sink down in a drift."

"I had an idea, Mom," Doug said. "Could we make a cave in the drift, the one you can see from the door?"

"Well, I'm not sure it would work. The snow might be too fluffy." Then she put her foot on a rise and smiled and said, "The wind seems to have packed it solid. So why not? I have an idea too. I'll use some of the jugs of water I stored up. Sprinkle it over the top. I may have to stand on the stepstool. It'll soon freeze and you'll have an ice roof."

"Man! That's neat," Craig said.

The boys played outside for nearly two hours. They stopped to go in the house a few times to change wet gloves for dry ones and warm their numb feet. They used a dustpan and a small snow shovel to scoop snow from the side of the drift toward the back door. "The problem," Doug said as they began to scoop, "is where are we going to put this snow? There's already plenty everywhere."

Craig looked around. "The only place is in the path out to the lane. Would it hurt to fill it up you suppose?"

"I don't see why. If no one can get up the lane, there won't be anyone to walk in the path."

"I'm going to let Scamp out," Doug's mother said after they'd made a place big enough for one boy to crawl in and sit down. They knew because Craig had tried it. He was smaller. "He hears you boys and doesn't want to be in here. Watch him now!"

Scamp ran in and out of the snow cave, getting in the way of the shovel and scoop and running between the boys' legs. Then he sat down and watched. His tongue hung out as he panted. "How can he be hot on a day like this?" Doug asked.

"He's probably just out of breath. I am too."

"*Your* tongue's not hanging out."

When the cave was large enough for both boys to sit upright and have some room to move around they decided to quit shoveling. "If we make it too big it might cave in."

Scamp's tongue hung out as he panted.
"How can he be hot on a day
like this?" Doug asked.

converse

"That sounds funny," Craig said. "A cave caving in."

Doug went to the door and asked if they could have a rug to sit on. "Snow might melt if we sat very long."

They talked after they settled themselves on the red and black rug. "It's like an igloo, I guess," Craig said. "The Eskimo houses. Only not so big."

"And we don't have to crawl through a snow tunnel to get in."

"I don't think I'd like that," Craig said. "I'd feel trapped."

"Maybe I would too. But if that's the only way we could keep warm, I guess that's what we'd have to do."

"Hey," Craig said. "I forgot about Scamp. Looks like he'd be in here with us before now. I'm going to get out and call him."

When Doug crawled out of the snow cave he saw Craig on top of the pile of snow they'd scooped into the path. "Look at that crazy dog," Craig said. "He's up on your garage roof. He walked right on top of the drift. Come down here!" Craig turned to Doug. "Man! That looks like fun. But I guess we'd better not try it."

"I guess not. We're too big."

Chapter 7

THE BOYS drank hot chocolate as they let the heat from the stove take away the shivery feeling. "It's going to get very cold tonight," Doug's mother said. "Down to twenty degrees below zero. It's a good thing the wind has died down. That would make it even harder to keep warm."

"Are we going to stay back here?" Doug asked.

"Why? Are you tired of being penned up in one room?"

"No, I sort of like it," Doug said.

"Well, that's good. It'll be a while before a repair truck from the light company could get down to us. So why not be prepared for the worst until the roads are clear."

Doug began to feel sleepy. He looked at Craig as his head jerked to one side. "I guess being out in the cold makes our eyes go shut," he said.

"So! Why don't you crawl into your hallway beds and take a nap? Then if you wish you can stay up later and watch TV or play games. Regular hours don't seem quite as important in such an unusual time as this."

The next thing Doug knew about what was going on in the world he heard his mother say, "Boys, come to the window. You shouldn't miss seeing this."

Scamp pattered behind them as they went to the window at the end of the kitchen. "Horses," Doug said. "What are they doing? Where could they be going?"

"I can't imagine," his mother said.

"What's that they're pulling?" Craig asked.

"I do not know the answer to that question," Ann Hartley said. "It's a kind of wooden sled. Some people call it a mud boat. My father called it a stone boat because he hauled rocks off fields with it when the plow turned them up. Sometimes he used it in other ways, too."

"Boat's a funny-crazy word for something that goes on land," Craig said.

"I know."

They watched the horses as they moved across

and around drifts. "The driver's looking for the lowest places," Doug's mother said.

"That man's having a hard time staying on. The way that boat or sled keeps tipping, I'd rather walk."

"Not for long, you wouldn't," his mother answered. "Walking in deep snow is very tiring."

"Isn't it for the horses?"

"Yes, I'm sure it is. But the driver lets them rest. That's what they were doing when I glanced out the window, before I called you. I wonder, does anyone know why he's out this time of evening, when it's getting colder by the minute? I'm going to call someone, if their line's not busy."

As the boys watched, the big brown horses strained to get through the deep snow. They pulled the sled around the corner of a grove of trees and disappeared from sight.

"It's dark almost," Craig said. "Can horses see in the dark?"

"Some, I guess. People used to ride behind them or ride on them in the dark—like Paul Revere."

"And that other guy who rode with him. What was his name? I keep forgetting."

"Dawes," Doug said. "William Dawes. I wonder why the books don't say much about him? He went as far as Paul Revere—maybe farther."

"Yes. And how do we know Paul Revere would have gone by himself?" Craig said.

"Yeah, how do we? Maybe he was scared of the dark for all we know. He could have been. I'm not scared, but I'm going to turn on some lights."

As he walked to the light switch on the wall,

Doug heard his mother say on the phone, "How terrible. To think she was in pain all this time and wouldn't call anyone. . . . Well, I'd better feed these boys. Call me if you hear more. And if you can get through to me. . . . Oh yes! We're fine. Plenty of food and wood. No problems! Don't worry about us."

Before she could tell the boys who was in pain and why, the telephone rang again. "It's your father," she said to Doug. The boys heard the story of who the man with the horses was going to rescue as she told it over the telephone. "It's Mrs. Bartlett, who lives alone up on Road 700. She fell and broke her arm last night when a storm door blew open. She stepped out to pull it back and slipped." She went on to explain that the lady with the broken arm didn't call her children to tell them and hadn't said anything about being hurt when they called to check on her. "Why?" Ann said, "Because she didn't want them to risk their lives trying to get to her. I understand that. I'd feel the same."

As Doug's mother buttered bread for toasted cheese sandwiches she reported that some state highway plows had been seen on State Road 13. "If your dad hears that it's open to traffic, he'll go as far as he can. Then he'll come on home when other roads are open—or by *any* road he can find open to get here."

"Would he start out if it wasn't safe?" Craig asked.

"Do you know what my Dad did?" Craig asked. "He hired a plane and parachuted to an airport somewhere near here!"

N1872C
converse

"I doubt it. Besides, in most parts of the state people are warned or perhaps even ordered to stay off the roads."

"Cause it's not safe?"

"Or because cars which are stalled in the roads keep snowplows from doing their job."

Before bedtime they heard that the lady with the broken arm had been taken from her home on the snow boat to a doctor who'd ridden from the city on a snowmobile. They'd met at the home of a cousin where Mrs. Bartlett would stay until the roads were open. Then she could have the break checked at the hospital and come home again.

"Will the man with the horses come back this way?" Craig asked.

"I don't know," Ann Hartley said. "And I suddenly realize we don't know his name."

"Didn't Uncle John know?" Doug asked.

"No, he just said he was someone who'd moved to a farm east of here late last fall. He raises horses and shows them at state fairs."

"He must be a great guy," Craig said. "To help people around here when a lot of us don't even know his name."

Craig and Doug watched television for a long time. Most of the regular programs were back on the air again. But three times they were broken into by special news bulletins about the roads.

"I thought my mom might call," Craig said as Ann handed him a wooden bowl of buttered popcorn.

"She probably knows you're safe. And if she had anything new to tell, she would call."

"She might be about out of money," Craig said. "I heard her put dimes and nickels in when the operator said forty cents for the first three minutes. When it's about the first of the month she runs out. 'Specially times when she needs to buy extra food, like now."

When the eleven o'clock news came on, the boys decided to go to bed. As Craig buttoned the top of his pajamas, Doug's mother called to him and said, "This telephone call *is* for you."

"For me? This late?" After he said hello he listened for so long that Doug thought the person who called had been cut off or hung up. Then Craig said, "Sure Dad. I'll look for you. But how did you get to New Castle? They keep saying to stay off roads. Okay. I'll wait."

Craig sat down in the beanbag chair. "I don't know what to think. Do you know what he did? He hired a plane and parachuted to an airport somewhere near."

"Parachuted!"

"Yeah. He does that all the time now—for air shows. That's what Mom didn't like. Mostly that's what it was. Cause he was gone a lot."

"Wouldn't it cost a lot of money to hire an airplane?" Doug asked.

"Seems like it. Unless Dad knows someone—one of his buddies maybe. That's what Mom called his friends. Anyway, he's going to try to get out here tomorrow—some way, to take care of me."

Chapter 8

THE BOYS slept until nearly nine o'clock the next morning. Doug had stayed awake a long time after he heard Craig's breathing become slow and deep. Questions kept going around in his mind. *How was Craig's dad going to get out this far? Why didn't he have the airplane fly him over his house so he could have jumped there? Could be he wouldn't know how to get Craig from here to his home.*

Another thought kept Doug awake longer. *Was*

Craig's dad going to do anything about Mrs. Scott? Didn't he care if she got home or not or that she had to stay in the shelterhouse? It seems like he would, unless he's awful mad at her.

Doug had been awake awhile the next morning before he raised up his head. *Mom's frying bacon.* He reached across the mattress and shook Craig's foot. "You awake?"

"Now I am. Is it day already?"

"It's day. But not already. We've been asleep a long time."

"Okay, I'll get up. If my dad does get here, I want to be ready. Besides, maybe we could play outside awhile."

"We'll see. Mom might say it's too cold." Doug crawled across the beds and looked all around the kitchen. "Mom?" When she didn't answer he thought she might have gone to the front part of the house. He listened for footsteps. Then he noticed that her quilted red coat was gone from the hooks behind the door.

What's she doing outside? he thought as he rubbed a spot on the frosty glass of the top part of the door. He saw that his mother had shoveled a short path toward the back fence. She was throwing something onto the drifts—something for the birds.

He pecked on the glass and she turned and waved and came into the house. "I wonder if the winter birds like rolled oats," she said as she reached down to unbuckle her snow boots. "I guess we'll find out."

"I don't see any doing any eating."

"I've heard that they won't come to food for an

hour after it's scattered. They say it takes that long for them to get over being scared away. Now I'll finish your breakfast. One egg or two?"

Both boys said "two" at the same time.

"This weather makes us hungry," Ann Hartley said. "Or is it the snow shoveling? Or both?" As she dropped slices of honey-wheat bread into the slots of the toaster she said, "I'm trying not to let my hopes get built up too much, but I'm sure I heard a snowplow over toward the west. Some kind of motor at least."

"Do you suppose they'll get here today?" Doug asked.

"We can't count on it. They keep telling that the snow's so deep and heavy that many pieces of equipment are breaking down or getting stuck. You two tired of being snowbound?"

"I'm not," Craig said. "It's okay here, warm and lots of food and someone to play with besides Scamp. But—"

"But you're wishing your mother wasn't away," Ann Hartley said.

"Yeah. And my dad. But no use to think about *that.*"

The boys asked to play outside but were willing to wait when Doug's mother said, "The sun's up and by eleven o'clock it should be slanting on the back door. Now it's bitterly cold."

They watched television a while and then they played two games of Rack-o, each one winning one. "Want to play the tie breaker?" Doug asked.

"No. I'd as soon both of us be the same. Why does one person always have to be best, anyway?"

"I don't know."

After putting one pair of gloves on top of the other and letting Doug's mother zip their coats all the way up to their chins, they went to the door. "Could we walk on the drifts today, Mom? If we stay where you can see us?"

She smiled and patted Doug's cheek. "Go ahead. I know how tempting those white mountains must be. The snow's hardpacked by the wind and the cold. It's safe."

"How do you know, Mrs. Hartley?" Craig asked.

She touched Craig's face with both hands. "Because I tried it—from the highest drift in the lane. I felt like a giant."

The boys hurried across the snow-filled path in the carport and walked up one drift and down another. "Look at the house," Doug said when they'd gone as far as the road. "It seems different, smaller, when I look down on it."

"A little like things do when you're in an airplane."

"You been in one?"

"Sure. More than once. When my dad lived with us. Before Mom got mad about his skydiving—or scared. I'm not sure which."

"Did you like flying?"

"Yes. It was okay. I wasn't scared. Well, maybe a little at first. I pretended I was a kite. I was only five, so I don't remember too much. Just about pretending I was a kite."

As the boys reached the top of the highest drift, Doug turned around and looked in all four directions. "As far as we can see, we could walk on snow.

'Cept on places like the other side of the row of bushes. They held about all the snow on one side."

"Where will all this go when it melts?" Craig asked.

"The newsman on television talked about that while you were on the phone with your dad last night. Some will soak in the ground but most will go into rivers. He said we might have a flood."

"We don't live close to a river, so I guess we don't have to worry about that," Craig said. "Hey, I forgot about Scamp. Where did he go?"

"Last time I saw him he was sniffing in the snow in the lane, as if he'd found some rabbit tracks."

"Here, Scamp! Here, Scamp!" Craig called, cupping his hand at the side of his mouth to make the sound go farther. He stopped calling and listened. "I think I hear him barking up toward our house."

"Do you think he'd try to get home?"

"He might. What I'm worried about is that there's no warm place for him to get in anywhere up there."

"Say!" Doug said. "Listen. I hear something—like a tractor."

"Yeah, but it's a different sound than any tractor I've ever heard. Could be a snowplow."

The boys stood still and listened some more. Craig said, "It's coming closer. I can tell. And there's Scamp, going along the top of a drift this side of the bend in the road."

"I see him. Look, Craig! That's a bulldozer. Someone's plowing us out!"

"It's not from the same place as other snowplows," Craig said. "It's not painted orange. What do you—that man, do you see what he's doing? He's getting off and picking up Scamp!"

Would a man who was plowing out a road stop to steal a dog? Doug thought. Before he could say this to his friend, Craig started running. As Doug watched, the man stood up, took off his red cap, and waved it back and forth in the air.

"That's my Dad!" Craig said as he slowed down and turned. "Come on."

I don't think I'll go, Doug thought. *I don't know Mr. Scott very well. He didn't sound friendly on the telephone. Besides, he and Craig will be talking. They won't need me around.*

Doug walked up the drifted lane and into the house. His mother turned from the window. "Do you suppose that's—"

"It *is* Craig's dad. He said so."

They're still coming. I thought maybe he'd back out."

"He probably wants to get Craig's things."

"Well, probably. I'll make some coffee. Mr. Scott's come a long way."

Craig reached the house before his father. Scamp scampered across the floor behind him. "My dad did come, Mrs. Hartley," Craig said. "Like he promised."

"That's fine. Tell him to come in."

"He's sweeping snow from his boots."

Doug's mother walked to the door and said, "Come in out of the cold. Don't worry about the snow."

"Well, I can only stay for a minute," Craig's father said as he took off his cap with the funny

Converse

eartabs. Doug noticed that the tall man's hair was the same color as Craig's, sort of like caramel icing on his mother's cakes.

"Take time for a cup of hot coffee," Ann Hartley said. "While Craig gathers up his things."

"I didn't bring much," Craig said. "Mainly just Scamp and myself. There wasn't much room on that snowmobile."

"I see him. Look, Craig! That's a bulldozer. Someone's plowing us out!"

Chapter 9

DOUG felt a little lonely as his friend got ready to leave. *Before he's gone I miss him. How can that be?*

"It's hard for me to say what's on my mind," Craig's father said as he slapped his red cap against his legs. "A person don't like to think how bad things might be for this boy if you hadn't got him to your place."

"Well, we did, and we're glad of it. You and Virginia would have done as much for Doug if there'd been a need."

"Ginny maybe," Craig's father said. "Not me. I'd have been off somewhere's playing around with my parachuting. Seems like it takes some folks longer to grow up than others. This blizzard—well, it hurried my growing up. I'd been putting too much on the shoulders of the boy's mom. If I'd been around close she wouldn't have needed to leave to get food. I mean to stay closer by from now on."

"You've talked to Virginia then?" Ann Hartley asked.

"Yep. She rode out from New Castle with me on the bulldozer—with as much food as we could manage to hold on to."

"You mean Mom's home *now?*" Craig asked.

"Yes she is. If my guess is right she's watching out the window right now to see if you're coming."

"Wow. I'm ready. Come on, Scampie. We're going home." Craig reached down for his dog then he raised up and walked over to Doug and his mother. "I'm glad Mom's okay and everything but it's been real great here. It wasn't scary or cold or anything bad."

"That's the way we wanted you to feel," Ann Hartley said.

"I reckon offering pay wouldn't be the thing to do," Craig's father said.

"No," Ann said as she smiled and patted Craig's cheek.

"No amount of money would be enough anyhow. Ready, son?"

"Ready." Craig looked at Doug. "Call me, okay?

Maybe we could walk in the drifts or play in the cave."

"Okay."

After they were alone, Doug pulled the beanbag chair closer to the stove.

"The house is quiet, isn't it?" his mother said.

"Yes it is. Mom, about Craig's dad—do you think he'll ever come back and live with Mrs. Scott and Craig?"

"I don't know. All he really said was that he meant to live closer."

"Craig seemed real happy, as if that was good enough."

"Perhaps it's better than he expected."

"I guess. He said, last night I think it was, that there's no use to think about his dad being around much."

Before the afternoon was over, Doug's father had called and said he was as far as Elwood. "The snow-plows would lose a race with a snail," he said. "*If* a snail could go more than a mile an hour. If the wind doesn't come up things may open up faster."

"Will you carry some wood in from the back porch?" Doug's mother said as she left the telephone. "I think I'll make a blackberry pie. I have some berries in the freezer. They're left from those we picked along the fencerow when we visited my Aunt Mae."

"We've used a lot of wood, Mom. Do you think we need the stove fire now? Should we save it?"

"I think we'll keep it going for tonight at least. It's supposed to get down to fifteen below zero. You know I like having a place to burn wrapping paper and boxes. I've been thinking I'll try to get one of those long-pronged newspaper log makers."

"*When* we get out, you mean."

"When we get out. Right."

"Are we going to eat any of that pie?" Doug asked later as they sat down to eat supper. "Or are you saving it for Dad?"

"Some of it. You don't think I'd refuse to let you eat a piece now, do you?"

As Doug looked across the table and smiled, the lights flickered, and then came back on. "Should we run some water?"

As his mother hurried toward the bathroom the lights went out. "I'm afraid it's already too late," she said. "But I filled all the jugs while you and Craig were out on the snowdrifts. And a pitcher of water for drinking is in the refrigerator."

She went carefully to the kitchen desk and carried the glass coal-oil lamp to the table. She struck a blue tip match against her shoe sole and held it to the woven strip which ran from the oil to the gold-colored burner. A fan-shaped flame threw a circle of light around the table.

"Why would the lights go out now?" Doug asked. "The wind's not blowing."

"We'll find out," his mother said. "The word will spread over the telephone. That makes me think! I can, and should, call the light company and report that we have no electricity."

"Want me to carry the lamp over there?"

"No, it's sort of top-heavy. The last thing we need is a fire."

"Mom! You put up the stove so we'd *have* a fire."

"True. But in the right place, where it can be controlled."

She lit a candle and found the right telephone number. After she'd given her name and address she listened for a minute or more before blowing out the candle and coming back to the table. "A pole's broken off over this side of the state road. A big payloader—What's a pay loader?"

"It's like a snowplow, only it scoops and dumps snow or sand or dirt over on another place."

"Well, it got too close to a pole and snapped it off."

"Will the lights be off a long time?"

"The man said it will take quite a while because they need to call a repair truck in from some other place."

Doug pulled a blanket from the mattress bed, folded it, and laid down behind the stove. *I'm curled up like Scamp,* he thought. *He's a good little dog. Having him here didn't make me miss Ott more. He's been dead too long for that. But I'd sort of like to have a dog of my own again.*

His mother pulled a rocker close to the stove and carried the lamp from the table to the kitchen desk. Doug watched as she sat down and opened a book. "You going to read by that light?"

"Yes, people did for years and years. And so did I until I was nine."

"I think I'll try it. I've never read by a coal-oil lamp."

Doug began to feel sleepy after he'd read two chapters in his mystery story. He couldn't stay awake until he got to the place where it told who was living in the deserted log cabin. *And I won't peek. That would spoil the story.*

"Mom," he asked as he came back from the bathroom after changing into pajamas, "how'd you know all those things to do, to get ready for the blizzard? Like water jugs and wood and living and sleeping in one room?"

"Well, we had bad storms when I was growing up. One was as bad as this. And I saw my mother doing what I did, except she didn't need to fill jugs with water. We had a pump—a hand-powered pump at the kitchen sink."

"Were you scared—then I mean?"

"No, I don't remember that I was. It all seemed exciting. I often remember the time when ice coated the snow-covered fields and all the children in the neighborhood tied sleds one behind the other. It was so smooth one person could pull seven sleds and do what we called crack-the-whip, whirl around and make the sleds go in a circle. The one on the end went the farthest and the fastest. The person on it often fell off. I never would ride on the end."

"Were you afraid this time?" Doug asked.

"What do you think?"

"I think you were a little. Your eyes had sort of a scared look when the wind shook the house."

"I didn't hide my feelings too well."

"You did okay. I wasn't scared."

"Good. I think the difference is that I was responsible for taking care of things. At your age I saw the adventure. My parents felt as I have this time."

The wood in the stove crackled and a spark flew out of the air slots below the door. Doug felt safe and warm.

"How would you like—" his mother started.

"I know what you're going to say. How would I like a cup of hot chocolate? I'd like it fine."

Chapter 10

DOUG'S mother slept on the mattress which had been Craig's bed. "With no electricity, I couldn't keep warm in the den," Ann Hartley said. "My mother would have heated bricks or stones on the stove. We took them to bed with us."

"Didn't they burn your feet?"

"No, Mom wrapped them in newspapers. I can still remember the smell, a mixture of bricks and newspapers."

The room was warm when Doug went to sleep and he didn't open his eyes until he realized he was reaching for a blanket. Almost at the same time the radio came on with a roar.

"Oh, my goodness," Doug's mother said. "I must have left that on and brushed against the knob when I reached for matches."

"I guess that means the lights are back on," Doug said. "Why is it cold?"

"Because the lights came on just now and the fire's died down. I only got up once in the night."

When the room was warm Doug decided to take a bath before he dressed. He heard the telephone above the rush of the water. He turned the knob of the faucet and heard his mother say, "Now that's good news, Charles. You think you'll be here by noon then. . . . Really! You feel we can get out—go to the store. . . . Oh, no. We're not out of anything. We're low on eggs, but not out."

Doug hurried with dressing. "I heard. Dad's coming."

"Yes, he's in Muncie. He'll follow the snowplow out State Road 3. Then he'll take the path Mr. Scott made with the bulldozer."

"How'd Dad—oh, I forgot we told him last night."

Ann Hartley walked to the south window. "The sun's bright already. Come here, Douglas. Do you see who's coming up the road?"

"Yeah, that's Craig and his mother. He's carrying

Doug reached out and took the light tan dog and held it close. "It's shivering," he said.

converse

something. Probably Scamp."

"Well—perhaps."

When Craig came to the back door Doug was there to open it. He looked out the window first. "That's not Scamp. That dog's not near as big as Craig's."

"Hey, come in. Where'd you find that little rascal?"

"I didn't. My Dad did. He brought it back last night—for you, if you want him."

Doug looked at his mother who was smiling and nodding her head. He reached out and took the light tan dog and held it close. "It's shivering," he said.

"Sure. It's cold," Craig said. "Are you glad my dad went to the dog pound last night and made them open up after closing time?"

"I sure am," Doug said.

"I think they were glad to get rid of another stray," Craig's mother said. "Like as not they've had several boarders this cold weather."

"Well, it was nice of Mr. Scott to go to all that trouble," Doug's mother said.

"You're right there," Mrs. Scott said. "He was real thankful to know you took care of our boy. Same as me."

Doug and Craig sat down on the end of one mattress and watched the long-haired dog sniff at the chair legs and around the stove. "I didn't tell Mom, but I know another reason my dad got the dog for you."

"What?"

"Cause. He saw how you kept petting Scamp's head while I gathered up my stuff. He said he could tell you were wanting a dog of your very own."

"I didn't know it for sure. Not until you went home. I was sad about Ott until now. Maybe I still am a *little*, but not so much."

"What you going to call him?" Craig asked.

"I don't know. What do you think?"

"Mom, when she made cookies this morning, used some powder the same color as he is. It was ginger, I think."

"Ginger! That's a great name. Come on over here, Ginger."

"Did you walk all this way to bring the dog to Doug?" Ann Hartley said as Virginia Scott stood up and started to the door.

"Mostly, yes. The rest of what's on my mind I could do on the telephone. That is to tell you how guilty I felt about going out that afternoon with the weather so bad and all."

"But you needed food."

"I did. But I could have planned better. I should have listened to the news. Instead I went back to bed. I didn't wake up until it was unsafe to be on the roads. Even after Craig's teacher called I thought I'd be back before the bus. That was real foolish."

"Well, it all came out all right," Ann Hartley said. "And for that matter, I have guilty feelings too. I could have called you when I went for food."

"Yes, but thanks to you it all came out all right. And something else good came out of this. It's Tom. He's grown up a lot. He said he was going to go back to work in the garage. So he'll be nearby to help out if we're in trouble. I tell you the truth, I was figuring on moving to the city before he said that."

"Mom!" Craig said. "You didn't tell me about moving."

"No, I put it off. I knew you wouldn't want to leave your school and Doug. But that's past."

"You think you could come to my house?" Craig asked as the boys went to the other end of the kitchen for water for the dog.

"I'll ask," Doug said. "My dad will be home about noon. Then they might go to town. I'd rather stay with you."

"Your dad coming in your car?" Craig asked. Before Doug could answer, Craig said, "Mom, where's our car? You didn't say."

"It's in the garage. That's how your dad got a job so quickly. A snowplow banged the Bug and when he called a tow truck they asked him to come back."

"That means you don't have a way to go," Ann Hartley said.

"That doesn't bother me. Not now. I had more than my share of being away."

"Well—I think we're going to the grocery store when Charles gets back. Make out a list of what you need."

"I don't need anything. Tom brought out two more sacks of groceries last night."

"Could I stay with Craig?" Doug asked.

"Looks like you boys would be tired of each other."

"I'm not tired of *him*," Craig said.

"Me neither. Can I bring Ginger?"

"Sure."

After Craig and his mother left, Doug's mother

said, "I'm going to move the mattresses back. We're supposed to have a warming trend."

"But are you going to leave the stove up?"

"Oh, yes, for the rest of the winter."

By twelve o'clock the kitchen was as it had been before the storm, except for the stove. The door to the den was opened and heat turned up there and in the bedrooms.

"It's almost like we hadn't had a blizzard," Doug said, "except for Ginger and the snowdrifts."

"And for Craig's father being closer," his mother said. "I'm sure Ginny is relieved."

"Seems like Craig was happy too," Doug said. "It's like that's the best thing for him—having his dad back in New Castle."

"Well, wouldn't it be for you?"

"No, I'd want my dad to be in the very same house."

"That's where we agree," his mother said. "Now, if you'll bring in some wood I'll start lunch. How does the idea of breaded tenderloin and macaroni and cheese hit you?"

"It hits me just right. I think I'll take Ginger to the den. Come on, dog. See where you live."

The dog gave three sharp yaps and followed Doug down the hall.

"Come on. Jump up here." As he ran a hand along Ginger's silky hair, Doug looked out the window. *I'll be able to see Dad when he drives in. We sure will have a lot to talk about. Ginger, and the horses taking Mrs. Bartlett to get her arm fixed. People were real nice to each other. Uncle John brought the wood even if he did nearly get stuck. And he came with Jeff on the snowmobile. I guess good things happen even in a blizzard.*

He saw a flash of red and called, "Mom, he's here. Dad's home. It's all okay now. You don't need to be scared any more, not now."

Dorothy Hamilton, a Selma, Indiana, housewife began writing books after she became a grandmother. As a private tutor, she has helped hundreds of students with learning difficulties. Many of her books reflect the hurts she observed in her students. She offers hope to others in similar circumstances.

Mindy is caught in the middle of her parents' divorce. *Charco* and his family live on unemployment checks. *Jason* would like to attend a trade school but his parents want him to go to college.

Other titles include: *Anita's Choice* (migrant workers), *Bittersweet Days* (snobbery at school), *The Blue Caboose* (less expensive housing), *Busboys at Big Bend* (Mexican-American friendship), *The Castle* (friendship), *Christmas for Holly* (a foster child), *Cricket* (a pony story), *Eric's Dis-*

covery (vandalism), and *The Gift of a Home* (problems of becoming rich).

Mrs. Hamilton is also author of *Jim Musco* (a Delaware Indian boy), *Ken's Hideout* (his father died), *Kerry* (growing up), *Linda's Rain Tree* (a black girl), *Mari's Mountain* (a runaway girl), *Neva's Patchwork Pillow* (Appalachia), *Rosalie* (life in Grandma's day), *Scamp and the Blizzard Boys* (friendship in a winter storm), *Straight Mark* (drugs), *Tony Savala* (a Basque boy), and *Winter Girl* (jealousy).

Four books of adult fiction by Mrs. Hamilton are also available: *Settled Furrows* and a trilogy on family relationships, *The Killdeer, The Quail,* and *Eagle.*

In addition to writing, Mrs. Hamilton has spoken to more than 100,000 children, mostly in school appearances in Indiana, Ontario, Pennsylvania, Tennessee, and Virginia.

"What's your favorite part in writing a book?" one young student asked.

"Right now, it's being here with you," she replied.

"The prospect of facing 80 fifth- and sixth-graders at the same time is enough to send many adults for the nearest exit," a news reporter noted, "but for Dorothy Hamilton it is pure delight."